Maua and the Garden of Plenty

Written by Linda Omare

Illustrated by Chike Obasi and Emmanuel Adepitan

First published 2022 by Kunda Kids Ltd

A catalogue record for this book is available from the British Library.

ISBN 978-1-7397269-0-4

MAUA

AND THE GARDEN OF PLENTY

Maua and the Garden of Plenty is an inspiring children's story that demonstrates the power of a big idea, however small you are! Join Maua on a journey of a lifetime to save her people and teach them a valuable lesson about resilience and self-confidence.

About Linda Omare

Linda Omare is a Kenyan children's book author, and Co-founder of 2nacheki, Africa's leading Pan-African media production company. Linda is a multi-talented creative who is passionate about storytelling.

About 2nacheki

2nacheki, pronounced (tu-na-cheki) which means 'we are watching' in Swahili slang, is a Pan-African media production company. 2nacheki reaches millions of people around the world with a fresh and authentic African perspective.

About Kunda Kids

Kunda Kids is an award-winning children's publishing and media production studio with a single purpose: **to inspire the next generation of young people about African history and culture.**

'Maua and the Garden of Plenty' is a creative collaboration between 2nacheki and Kunda Kids in an effort to bring fun, progressive and inclusive stories to children across Africa and the rest of the world.

Once upon a time, in a small town called Azania,
there lived a teeny-weeny girl named Maua.

Maua was the last born in a big family and often felt ignored because of how small she was.

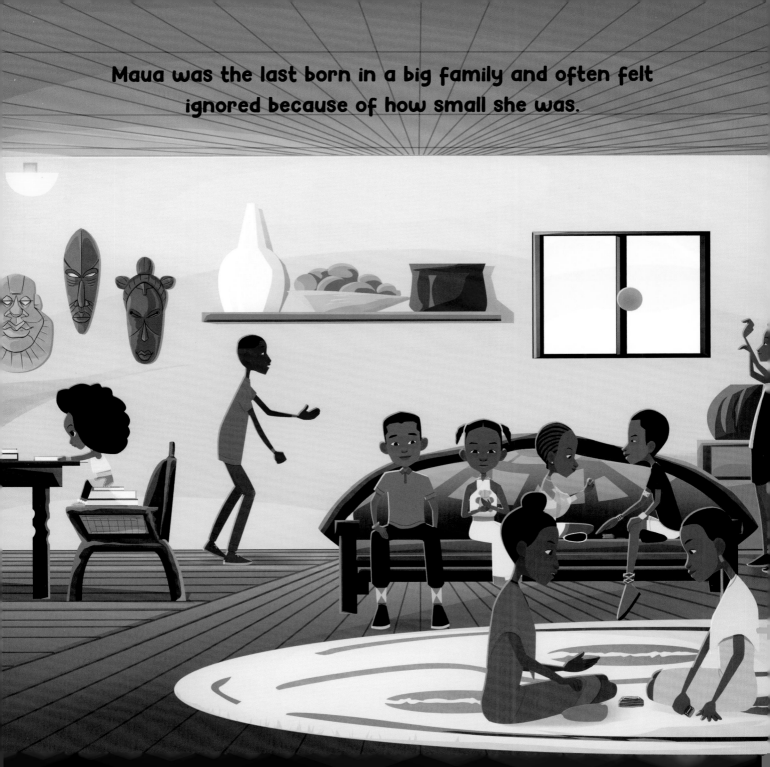

Every day, the Azanian people would tend to their gardens. The gods would reward them for their hard work with an abundance of delicious fruits and vegetables.

However, the Azanian people became lazy over time. They did less work and complained, yet still expected the gods to reward them with big juicy fruits and vegetables.

The gods became worried and decided to teach them a lesson. The less work the Azanian people did, the fewer fruits and vegetables the gods gave them.

Eventually, the gardens became empty, and the Azanian people became hungry.

They pleaded with the gods to forgive them,
but their baskets remained empty for many weeks.

One morning, Maua woke up early so she could be ready first.

For Maua, being small in a big house was tough. To avoid being squeezed out of the kitchen and bathroom, she learned how to think ahead.

It was time for Maua and her family to head to the gardens. On the way, Mama asked, "My dear children, what can we do to please the gods and have delicious food again?"

Each of the siblings had an idea, including Maua, but no one wanted to hear what she had to say.

Maua let out a big sigh. Mama noticed and asked, "Maua, tell me, what do you think?"

Maua was happy to be heard and replied, "I think we should start planting our food to show we understand the importance of hard work and are thankful for what we have."

Mama smiled and said, "This is a great idea!" Mama knew Maua had a big heart and a bright mind.

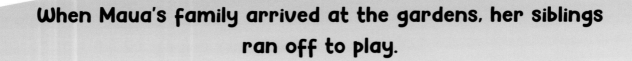

When Maua's family arrived at the gardens, her siblings
ran off to play.

Meanwhile, she looked for a shovel and began to dig into the soil.

Everyone laughed that such a small girl would be digging.

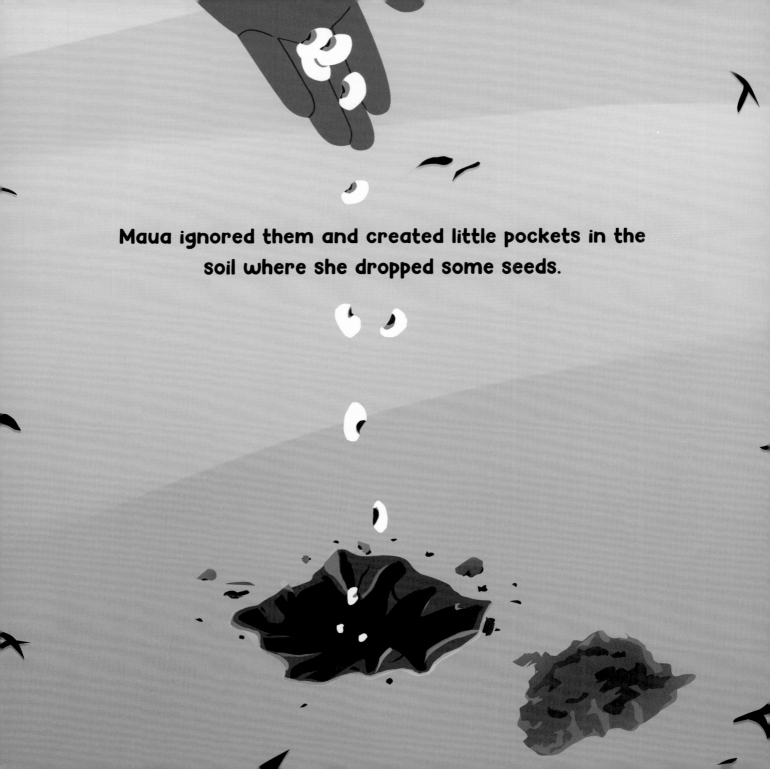

Maua ignored them and created little pockets in the
soil where she dropped some seeds.

She did this every day, and each time people
laughed, until one day, Mama joined in.

Over time, the gardens were full of sprouting fruits and vegetables and the promise of a new harvest. Soon, other villagers joined Maua to plant more food.

The gods were pleased that Maua helped everyone understand the importance of hard work. The gods made the crops grow faster, bigger, and more delicious than ever before to reward the people.

Eventually, the Azanian people's baskets were overflowing with fruits and vegetables, and the gardens looked beautiful again.

One morning, Maua and her family heard the noise of a large crowd outside their home.

The Great Chief of Azania walked through the crowd and towards Maua and Mama.

She opened her right hand to reveal a small crown made of gold. The whole town marvelled at the shining object as she placed it on Maua's head.

She announced, "This girl saved our people from a terrible disaster, and she is very special."

The chief turned to face the crowd and said, "This is a lesson, that none of us can ever be too small to make a big difference."

The crowd rejoiced and celebrated Maua with a traditional Azanian dance.

Maua was pleased that she was able to help her people and life at home with her big family became much better too!